Jermaine
The Dawning

Story: Jacob McFadden
Cover Design: Jacob McFadden
www.jacobmcfadden.info
© 2024

Table of Contents

Chapter 1

It's a rainy afternoon in Joeman City. Reginald Osei, a construction worker, and his wife Patricia are waiting in the doctor's office for the ultrasound results of their unborn son. Dr. Tryune enters, but has a look of sadness as he stands in front of them. "Mr. and Mrs. Osei, I'm afraid that I have some unpleasant news. The ultrasound revealed fractures and deformities in your son's skeletal system. He has a severe form of Brittle Bone Disease and won't live long."

"What?" says Reginald. Patricia, who has profound deafness, reads the low countenance on her husband and doctor. "Is our baby ok?" she signs. Reginald has tears in his eyes and signs to her what the doctor said. Patricia is shocked and tears up. "There's still hope." "What do you mean?" "I'm working on a cure, but it's not perfected yet. See a year ago my son had the disease and died shortly after he was born." "And your wife?" "She died from complications of the delivery." Reginald gulps.

"What's going on Reginald?" "The doctor is working on a cure." A somewhat sigh of relief comes over her face. "When will the cure be available?" "The doctor doesn't know." "I'll continue to work on this until something breaks through. Hopefully soon."

***

Dr. Tryune is in his lab. He mixes liquids together in a flask. With a syringe, he feeds the cure to the mice that have the disease. Later, he looks at the X-rays but is disappointed because there's no improvement in their deformities. He continues to work on the cure.

Two weeks pass, and there's still no improvement. He sits at his desk with beads of sweat on his face because of the amount of pressure he's under. Nevertheless, he continues to try.

Four days later, he feeds the mice the cure and takes X-rays. To his astonishment, the bones of the mice are now normal. A sigh of relief comes over his face.

***

Reginald is serving Patricia breakfast in bed. The phone rings. "Hello?" "Mr. Osei, I need to see you and your wife as soon as possible."

***

"The formula for the cure finally worked. I tested it on the mice and lo and behold their fractures and deformities have healed. I also tested it on the normal mice and there was no effect...But I don't know the outcome it has on humans yet...With that being said, it's a chance we are going to have to take...Since your son is still in the womb...the only way to get it to him is through your wife." Reginald turns to Patricia and explains it to her.

Now Patricia is alarmed. He turns to Dr. Tryune. "Doc I'm scared." "I understand, but this is the only shot we've got." Reginald is conflicted. Patricia puts her hand on Reginald's shoulder. "Let's do this." Reginald's face turns into a smile. He turns to Dr. Tryune. "Let's do it." Dr. Tryune hands Patricia the bottle. Patricia holds the bottle up to her lips and mentally prepares herself before she drinks it.

***

One week has passed. The sonographer rubs the stethoscope over Patricia's belly while the baby is on the monitor.

***

Reginald and Patricia are sitting and waiting on the results. In comes Dr. Tryune. "Mr. and Mrs. Osei, you have a healthy baby boy. "Reginald's eyes light up with delight. He turns to Patricia. "Our boy is healthy!!" Patricia starts to shed tears of joy. "Thanks Doc," as he shakes Dr. Tryune's hand.

***

Six months later…
It's the middle of the night. Patricia and Reginald are in bed asleep. Patricia wakes up and starts moaning with her hands on her stomach. Reginald wakes up and is concerned. "It's that time," Patricia signs. Reginald immediately grabs the phone and dials. "Doc my wife's going into labor!"

***

Patricia is lying on the bed in the delivery room, and Reginald is there by her side. Dr. Tryune along with the nurse deliver the baby. They all notice that the baby is not breathing. Dr. Tryune checks the baby's heart. "There's no heartbeat!" Everyone is shocked. Dr. Tryune grabs the manual defibrillator and immediately uses it on the baby, but after several attempts the baby is still lifeless.

Dr. Tryune is breathing heavily and turns to Reginald and Patricia in sorrow. Patricia weeps and shakes her head in disbelief. Reginald has tears in his eyes while he holds Patricia. But while everyone is having their all is lost moment, the baby starts to cry. Dr. Tryune and the nurse rush over to the baby.

Dr. Tryune checks the baby's heartbeat, and a sigh of relief comes over his face. "His rhythm is normal." A sigh of relief comes over Reginald's and Patricia's face. The nurse wraps the baby in a blanket and carries him to Reginald and Patricia. Patricia holds the baby. "What do you want to name him?" signs Reginald. Patricia hands the baby to Reginald and signs, "Jermaine."

***

Two days later...
Patricia is lying in bed and holding Jermaine. Reginald is standing beside her while Jermaine is holding on to his index finger. In comes Dr. Tryune. "All of the tests came back negative...You all are free to go."

***

Later that night…

4

Dr. Tryune is sitting on his bed and updating his notes about the cure on his laptop. When he's done, he looks over at the clock. 11:30 p.m. it displays. He now has the munchies but is contemplating on whether or not he should satisfy his cravings.

***

Dr. Tryune enters the convenience store and walks to the back. He grabs a bag of potato chips. As Dr. Tryune gets ready to go to the front counter, the cashier is being held at gunpoint by a man in a black ski mask. A silencer is on the muzzle. "Give me all of it." "You don't have to do this." The man pulls the trigger and the bullet enters the cashier's forehead.

Dr. Tryune does a hammer fist to the man's wrist which causes the gun to fall out. He does a sidekick to the man's ribs, and the man falls to the ground. The man pulls out the gun that's attached to his ankle and shoots Dr. Tryune in the chest. He walks over to Dr. Tryune and takes Dr. Tryune's wallet. He runs out of the store.

***

The man is in his car and in a secluded area. He takes off his mask and looks through Dr. Tryune's wallet. He takes the money out and finds a picture of Dr. Tryune with his wife. Since he doesn't know that she's deceased, he decides to take her out as well. He looks at the address on Dr. Tryune's driver's license.

***

The man knocks on the door while keeping his other hand in his coat pocket to conceal the gun, but no one answers. The man goes back to his car and lights a Molotov cocktail. He throws it into Dr. Tryune's window. The robber quickly gets back into his car and drives off. Dr. Tryune's room becomes engulfed in flames and the information about the cure is now lost.

***

The next morning Reginald and Patricia are eating breakfast at the table and baby Jermaine is in the crib. The news anchor comes on the TV. "Physician and founder of Hopewell Hospital has died. Dr. Ralph Tryune was murdered at Tim's Convenience Store late last night. Coincidentally, his house was also burned down. No casualties were found in the fire." Reginald and Patricia are shocked and saddened by this.

***

Days later, Reginald, Patricia and baby Jermaine along with others attend the funeral.

***

A year has passed...
Reginald and Patricia are sitting on their living room couch. A commercial comes on displaying a husband, wife and their son and daughter. The countenance on Patricia drops. "Honey what's wrong?" "I want to have another child, but I'm scared." Reginald sighs and hugs her. "I know how you feel because I feel the same way." "I was thinking about us adopting."

"Adopting huh?" Patricia nods. Reginald thinks about it for a moment. "You know that's not a bad idea. In fact, it's the only choice we have if we're going to play it safe." Patricia smiles.

***

The next day Reginald calls the adoption agency to set up his and Patricia's profile.

***

5

A week goes by, and Reginald gets a call from the adoption agency. "Mr. Osei, your family has been chosen to adopt."

***

Nine months pass...
Reginald is on the phone with a representative from the agency. Reginald's countenance drops as he listens to her over the phone. After Reginald gets off of the phone, he turns to Patricia. "She decided to keep the baby." Patricia's countenance drops as well. It's a bittersweet moment for the both of them.

***

Three months later, Reginald gets a call from the adoption agency and a smile comes over his face as he's speaking. He hangs up the phone. "We have a baby girl." Tears fill Patricia's eyes as she smiles. "What do you want to name her?" he signs. "Nia, we'll name her Nia."

***

Four months later, they stand before a judge in court to finalize the adoption.

***

Six years later...
Jermaine and Nia are sitting with Patricia at a little table at the outlet mall. Jermaine is coloring in a coloring book and Patricia is telling kids stories to Nia by sign language. As Jermaine looks up from coloring, he notices a young man with a small box behind his back talking to a young woman. Jermaine becomes curious and instinctively uses his transparent vision. There's a ring in the box. The man gets on one knee and proposes to the woman. He shows her the ring. The woman is excited and nods. She hugs the man. Jermaine smiles.

Three men wearing motorcycle helmets and baggy dark gray trench coats pass by. Jermaine becomes curious about what is under their coats. He uses his transparent vision. They're carrying sawed-off shotguns. Jermaine's face goes from smiling to confused. The three men cross the street and enter the jewelry store. Patricia looks at her watch. "We gotta go pick up your dad."

***

Later that night...
Patricia is putting up the dishes. As she walks out of the kitchen, the 10 o'clock news comes on the TV. She is shocked by the headline "ROBBERY AT JOEMAN'S PREMIUM STORE OUTLETS." Closed captioning is being shown as the anchor man speaks. "Rueben's Jewelry Store located at the Joeman Premium Store Outlets was robbed earlier today." Jermaine is in bed listening from his room.

"Three men wearing motorcycle helmets and gray trench coats entered the store. One of the robbers held the owner at gunpoint while the others took the store's most valuable possessions. The police are further investigating the incident."

***

Patricia goes into Jermaine's room to make sure he's in bed. She notices that he has a sad look on his face. "Jermaine, what's wrong?" "I was able to see the guns those men were hiding before anybody else could?" "What guns? Wait, are you talking about the robbery today?" "Yes." "What do you mean by seeing them before anyone else? Was part of the gun sticking out? Was there a hole or an imprint of the gun?"

6

"No, it was none of that. I was able to see clearly inside of their coats." "Jermaine, I have no idea what you're talking about." "I can prove it…Go grab something small and put it in your hand, but don't let me see it."

***

While still being confused, Patricia leaves and opens her purse that's on the couch. She grabs a quarter.

***

As she comes back into Jermaine's room, her hands are hanging down by her sides. One of them is in a fist. She points to her fist with the other hand. Jermaine uses his transparent vision. "It's a quarter." Patricia is shocked. "Wait here." She rushes back into the living room.

***

Patricia grabs a penny out of her purse and goes to her bedroom.

***

Reginald is in bed asleep, and Patricia shakes Reginald until he comes awake. "Put this in your hand and don't let Jermaine see it." Reginald is confused, but he takes the penny. Patricia grabs him by the wrist and drags him out of bed. They enter Jermaine's room.

***

"Remember, don't show Jermaine." Reginald nods. "Jermaine, what's your dad holding in his hand?" Jermaine uses his transparent vision. "A penny." Reginald opens his hand and is shocked as he briefly looks at the penny. "Son how did you do that?" "I don't know exactly…I just focus my eyes and do it." Reginald signs to Patricia what Jermaine said.

"When did you notice you could do this?" she signs. "Today." Reginald turns to Patricia. "Are you thinking what I'm thinking?" "The cure," she signs. "What cure?" Reginald and Patricia look at each other. Reginald tells Jermaine the story.

Chapter 2

Five years later...

Jermaine is now in the 7th grade and it's the third week of school. Jermaine is washing his hands in the restroom. Brent, his two friends Andrew and Lincoln, are also in the restroom. Andrew and Lincoln are washing their hands while Brent is putting toilet paper from the stalls into his backpack. "Hey man, what's with the toilet paper concealment?" asks Andrew. "I'm helping my old man save money since we're low on cash."

As Brent continues to put the toilet paper in his backpack, the janitor walks in. "You put that back, or I'm reporting you." Brent puts all of the toilet paper back in the stalls. Brent, Lincoln, Andrew and Jermaine head towards the restroom door. Brent holds the door open for Jermaine.

"After you," says Brent. As Jermaine walks out, Brent sticks his foot out on purpose, causing Jermaine to trip and fall. Andrew and Lincoln laugh. "Watch your step," says Brent as he passes by Jermaine. Jermaine angrily gets up and carries on.

***

As the janitor is mopping the hallway, Ms. Evans walks by. "Good morning...How's it going?" "Oh it's going alright...Just caught a youngster stealing toilet paper out of the restroom." Ms. Evans sighs and has an epiphany. *That's probably why my chalk went missing Friday morning.* "When are these kids gonna learn some ethics?" says the janitor. "Oh I totally agree with you." The janitor shakes his head as he continues to mop.

***

Ms. Evans enters her classroom and sets her book satchel on the table. She pulls out her math book and planner and sets them on the table as well. She pulls out her box of chalk. *I better put these away.* As she puts her hand on the desk drawer handle, she's interrupted by a history teacher.

"Ms. Evans, there's no chalk in my room. Can I have a few pieces of yours? I'll pay you back tomorrow." "Sure." She hands him four pieces of chalk. The principal walks in. He has a thick southern drawl. "Ms. Evans, I need to see ya in my office for a minute." "Sure Mr. Berkman."

Ms. Evans forgets to put the chalk in the drawer and lays it on top of the desk. Moments later, Brent walks into the classroom and grabs it.

8

***

Brent locks himself in a restroom stall. He pulls out a piece of chalk and eats it. The bell for first period rings. Brent puts the chalk back in the box and puts the box in his coat pocket. He heads off to class.

***

The students along with Brent and Jermaine come in and take their seats. In comes Ms. Evans a few seconds later. "Good morning class. I hope you all had a good weekend, and I hope the homework wasn't too torturous." Ms. Evans chuckles, but the students stay quiet.

"Well, if there aren't any questions, pass in your homework." As everyone passes up their homework, Ms. Evans looks for her box of chalk. She looks in the desk drawers, underneath the book and planner and down on the floor. "Who stole my chalk!" The class stays quiet. "There was a box of chalk sitting on my desk…Who stole it!" Still no one says anything. "I know I'm not crazy." Brent raises his hand.

"Ms. Evans I have to go to the john." "No, nobody leaves this class." Brent gets out of his seat anyway. "Where are you going?" "I said I need to go to the john." Jermaine uses his transparent vision to scan Brent's coat pocket. "Brent has the chalk." Brent stops dead in his tracks, and all of the other students look at Jermaine.

"Empty your pockets Brent." Brent closes his eyes in frustration and pulls out the chalk. "You have two weeks detention starting tomorrow."

***

After school, Jermaine is walking home. Brent, Andrew and Lincoln run up on him from behind. Brent pushes Jermaine. "Hey!" Jermaine falls to his knees but gets back up. He angrily turns around. Brent steps in closer. "I don't like how you called me out today." "That was payback." Brent clocks Jermaine in the face. Jermaine falls to the ground again, and they start to kick him.

Ms. Evans drives up. She gets out. "Stop it!" Brent, Andrew and Lincoln run away. Jermaine is lying there bleeding from the cut that's over his eye. Ms. Evans helps Jermaine up. Jermaine gets in the car. She pulls out a first aid kit from the glove compartment and puts a bandage over his eye. "Let's get you home."

***

Patricia opens the door. Jermaine and Ms. Evans are standing there. "Jermaine! What happened to you?" "I got into a fight." Reginald comes to the door, and Patricia signs to him what happened. "Mr. Osei, he was jumped by some boys at school." Reginald is angry.

***

The next morning Jermaine, Ms. Evans, Patricia, Reginald, Brent, Andrew and Lincoln are in the principal's office. "I'm going to request that the superintendent expel these hoodlums for a year."

***

Later that afternoon, Jermaine sits on the couch as his parents have a discussion with him. "Son, you're mother and I have decided to enroll you in martial arts. We want you to learn how to defend yourself. We wanted to enroll your sister as well, but she's already involved in cheerleading. And we don't want to take that away from her. That means you are going to have to protect her." Jermaine nods.

***

9

The next afternoon Reginald, Patricia and Jermaine enter MASTER CHEN'S KUNG FU SAN SOO STUDIO. A Chinese man with a bald head and thick accent approaches them. "Hello, how may I help you?" "I've heard great things about San Soo, and I'd like to sign my son up," says Reginald. The man smiles.

"San Soo is fantastic. I've studied other disciplines in my day and learned from them all. But San Soo is my heart. I've been teaching it for over 20 years." "I see." "I'm Master Chen. My beginner classes are Monday, Wednesday and Friday from 5 to 7 p.m." Reginald smiles. "That's perfect."

***

The next day Jermaine begins his training.

Chapter 3

One year later...

Jermaine is walking in the hallway. A sign on the wall says, "TAEKWONDO TOURNAMENT AT TONE MIDDLE SCHOOL GYMNASIUM. COME SHOW WHAT YOU GOT."
Interesting.

***

Later that day, Jermaine is with Nia and Nia's friend at the mall. They walk by PHILLIP'S UNISEX CLOTHING STORE. "Oooo" says Nia and her friend as they stop and stare at the dresses in the window. "Very cool," says Nia. "Come on," as she motions to her friend. "I'll be out here," Jermaine says. Nia and her friend go into the store.

***

Jermaine sits on a bench across the way. Since he just bought a martial arts magazine, he pulls it out of the bag and starts to read it. He comes across an article that intrigues him. *Wow, I didn't know there was Taekwondo in the Olympics.* Jermaine starts to envision himself standing on a platform and receiving his gold medal.

***

While Jermaine is having his aha moment, Brent, Andrew and Lincoln are in the store as well. Brent notices Nia. "Hubba hubba." Andrew and Lincoln look over. "They're pretty cute," Andrew says. "Definitely," says Lincoln. "I got dibs on the chocolate one," says Brent.

***

"I'm definitely telling my parents I want these for my birthday," says Nia's friend. "You and me both." Brent approaches Nia. "Nice dress." Nia blushes. Her friend smiles and goes away. "I like your style. What's your name?" "Nia."

***

Jermaine raises his head up from reading. Brent and Nia are still talking. Jermaine is livid. He approaches them. "What do you say we go grab a bite to eat—" "Back off Brent she's too young for you." "Well look who it is…It's the snitch. Andrew and Lincoln approach Jermaine and stare him down. "You just stay away from my sister!"

Brent steps in closer to Jermaine. "You forgot... she won't be too young forever." Jermaine cocks his fist back. "You all take that outside. That'll be none of that in here," says the store manager in his thick Korean accent. "Come on Nia let's go." Jermaine, Nia, Nia's friend, Brent, Andrew and Lincoln leave the store.

***

"See you later fink!" Jermaine closes his eyes in irritation but ignores Brent's comment. He continues to walk with his sister and her friend.

***

The next day Jermaine arrives at the studio for his lesson. Master Chen is warming up. "Jermaine, you're here early." "Well Master Chen, I've been doing some thinking. Since you know about Taekwondo, I wanted to see if you would prepare me for the Olympics? There's actually a tournament happening at my school a month from now."

"Olympics? Hmm...A famous composer once said competitions are for horses, not artists. You should only be concerned about defending yourself on the street."

"Yes I get that Master Chen. It's just for me it would be a change of pace. You know something new to strive for." Master Chen thinks about it. "Well, I see where you're coming from, and I respect your desire. Since this is your goal, let's enter you into that tournament." Jermaine smiles.

"But first, you must know the rules." Jermaine nods. "Rule number one. Punches are only allowed to the body. Rule number two. Kicks are allowed to both the body and head, but...you must not kick with excessive force to the head. Only light, controlled kicks are allowed." "Got it Master Chen." Master Chen continues to tell him the rules.

***

A week before the tournament...

Jermaine is having dinner with his parents and sister. The enchiladas are off the chain ma," signs Jermaine. "So good," Nia signs. "They ain't lying," signs Reginald. Patricia is smiling. Reginald kisses Patricia on the cheek. Reginald goes back to his meal but stops and looks at Jermaine with admiration.

"My son is going to be trading blows next weekend." Jermaine smiles. "I'm a little nervous, but overall I feel pretty good." "I think you're going to do just fine," Patricia signs. "So do I," says Nia. "I appreciate all of the support. I'm so thankful Master Chen is helping me make this a reality—" The doorbell rings. Reginald gets up from the table.

***

He looks through the peep hole and opens the door. "Master Chen." Master Chen looks at Reginald with sad eyes. "I need to speak with Jermaine. This is for you all as well." Reginald lets Master Chen in.

"Y'all come on over here. Master Chen has something to say." Jermaine, Nia and Patricia get up from the table. "There's been a death in the family, and I will be leaving for Hong Kong tomorrow; therefore, I will not be at the tournament."

Jermaine is surprised. "Mr. Chen, I'm sorry for your loss, but I can't enter the tournament without a coach-" "Don't worry. I've taken care of that and you're still good to go." A somewhat sigh of relief comes over Jermaine's face. "Well, I have to get going." When Master Chen gets to the door, he turns around. "You will do well." Master Chen opens the door and leaves.

12

Chapter 4

Tournament Day

A crowd of people are in the bleachers. Jermaine watches the fighters before him. After a match is over, the referee announces the winner. Jermaine suits up since he's next. When Jermaine looks across the floor at his opponent, it's Brent. Brent smiles at him and Jermaine rolls his eyes. Brent walks over to Jermaine.

"We gotta stop meeting like this." Jermaine stares at Brent. "Fighters come to the center." "Well, let the best man win," says Brent. "Oh, and you're little sister...she's a real spreader if you know what I mean." Jermaine's eyes widen in surprise. Brent smiles and heads to the center of the ring. Jermaine is now enraged.

***

They get to the center of the ring and face each other. The referee calls out the commands. "Charyut." Jermaine and Brent continue to face each other. "Kyungrye." Brent bows but Jermaine doesn't out of anger. "That means bow," says the referee. Jermaine reluctantly bows. Brent and Jermaine turn their backs to the referee and do another bow. They turn back around and face each other. "Joon-bi." Jermaine and Brent get in their fighting stance. "Shijak!" Brent charges towards Jermaine. Jermaine delivers a spinning hook kick to Brent's face, knocking him up in the air and against the wall.

The crowd's in shock. Brent is lying face down and is unresponsive. Jermaine freezes in remorse for what he's done. The doctor, Brent's coach, and the referee rush to see about Brent. Reginald, Patricia, and Nia run up to Jermaine and pull him aside. "Son what happened?" "He taunted me dad and I lost it. And for some reason I felt...stronger than usual."

***

It's Monday morning and Jermaine and his parents are in the principal's office. "Brent's in a coma. He's suffered a broken jaw, a broken nose, a severe concussion and major damage to his spinal cord. Because of this incident, the Taekwondo Sanctions Committee has banned your son for life."

***

After the meeting, Jermaine and his parents walk to the car. "Mom, Dad...I need some time alone. I need to go for a walk." "We understand," Patricia signs. "Yeah son do what you have to do."

***

13

During Jermaine's walk, he walks by the studio. Master Chen is sweeping inside. Jermaine enters. "Master Chen, you're back." "What are you doing here? Didn't you get my message?" Jermaine checks his phone. "Oh my phone was off. I haven't checked it—" "You are not allowed here anymore!"

"What?" "I saw the video, and what you did at that tournament is a disgrace!" Jermaine's countenance drops. "The amount of power that you generated is mind-boggling. However, it's your lack of self-control that's at fault!" "Master Chen, he degraded my sister."

"It doesn't matter! You were supposed to stay calm and focused. I told you specifically what not to do and you did it anyway. You've wasted my time!" Jermaine becomes angry. "So it's like that huh?" Master Chen stares at Jermaine. "Alright…So be it." Jermaine leaves.

***

Jermaine arrives at his house and walks in with tears in his eyes. Jermaine sits on the couch and Reginald and Patricia sit with him. "Master Chen kicked me out because of the tournament." Reginald and Patricia are shocked and start to grieve even more. "He told me that I'm a waste of time. I'm such a failure." Patricia puts her hand on Jermaine's back to comfort him. "Aww son. I say we move away from this place and start over."

Patricia is surprised. "A few days ago a friend of mine who's now head of the construction department in McFade told me that a position just opened up, and it's mine if I want it. It pays more as well." "What if we encounter other issues?" signs Patricia. "Well…it's a chance we are going to have to take. Look, whatever we go through down there we'll get through it." Patricia nods and smiles. Reginald looks at his son. "What do you say Jermaine?" Jermaine smiles. "Let's do it."

***

A few days later, Reginald, Patricia, Jermaine and Nia are traveling on the highway. They pass by a sign that says, "WELCOME TO MCFADE CITY."

***

The next day, Jermaine is registering at his new school. He skims through the list of electives on the application. He's pondering on what to sign up for. He skims down further and his finger lands on band. He becomes intrigued and check marks it. Jermaine turns in the application and the admissions counselor looks it over.

"Were you in band last semester?" "No, I've never played an instrument in my life." "Our beginner's band is only in the first semester. The second semester is for more advanced students." Jermaine's countenance drops a little. "However, it's up to the discretion of the band director who he lets in. I'll talk to him."

***

The following day, the band director has a conversation with Jermaine. He has a thick southern accent. "Our sessions will begin an hour before school, and you can't miss any days unless it's absolutely legitimate. Ya hear me?" "I hear you sir." "Now, there's one caveat…All of the instruments are taken except the trombone." Jermaine's countenance drops. "I really wanted to play the saxophone." "Well son take it or leave it." Jermaine sighs. "I'll take it." "Alrighty, see ya bright and early."

***

Jermaine begins his lessons. He struggles to make a good sound on the trombone as he moves the slide up and down, but continues to take direction from the band director. As the weeks pass, Jermaine gets better and better and ends up becoming an exceptional player by the time he's in high school.

The Making of a Composer

Since Jermaine has mastered the trombone, he now wants to master song writing. He attends a jazz piano workshop the summer before his freshman year in college. "Today we're going to be learning how to finger the major scale," says the piano instructor. The piano instructor gives a demonstration. "Now these are weighted keys so you have to put some muscle into it when you press them."

Since Jermaine doesn't know that his strength has increased, he crushes the keys when he presses them. Jermaine is shocked and looks at his hands in embarrassment. While the instructor is helping another student, Jermaine moves to the next keyboard. As the piano instructor makes his way down the aisle, he's baffled because he notices the crushed keys. Jermaine doesn't say a word.

Chapter 5

Time has passed, and Jermaine is now a senior at Tayman University. He's in combo rehearsal with his classmates Donald Jackson (drummer), Michelle Wafers (bassist), Willie Peterson (pianist) and the combo director who is playing the bongos. The song comes to an end.

"Very nice tune Jermaine," says the combo director. "Yeah I was definitely feeling that," Willie says. "If anybody else wants to bring in any originals feel free." The rest of the band nods. "Well, it's about that time…I've got nothing else. See you all next week." The combo director leaves. Jermaine starts tearing down his trombone. "Hey, I've been wanting to talk to you all about something." "What's up," says Willie. "Since this is our last year in school, how about we become a band? An actual gigging band?"

Willie, Donald and Michelle briefly look at each other. "I'm down," says Willie. "So am I," says Michelle. "Count me in too," says Donald. Jermaine smiles. "What do you want to call us?" Donald asks. "Hmm, I don't know yet." "How about the Androgynous Jazz Project?" says Willie as he's nodding and smiling because he's really feeling that name.

Jermaine, Donald and Michelle have that "are you kidding me" look on their faces. Willie gets embarrassed and tries to shake it off. "Well you know…since we have a female in the group and all." "…How about Jermaine and the Band? I mean…since this is your idea," says Michelle. Willie nods. "I'm digging that." "Yeah, me too," says Donald. "Well alright…Jermaine and the band it is." "We're going to need a manager," Michelle says. "I know the perfect person."

***

Jermaine and Nia's Apartment

Nia is sitting at her desk. She's on her laptop computer writing a paper for one of her music management courses when she hears a knock at the door. She gets up and opens it. "Hey Nia…I got an offer for you," says Jermaine. "An offer?" "Yes…we are officially a band now, and we'd love for you to be our manager." "You'll get 20% of whatever we make."

"Wow that - that sounds great! I'd love to." "Awesome! Let's go celebrate." "Oh I can't…I have a test to study for tomorrow, and I work the entire weekend...How about next Friday?" "Next Friday works for me. How about y'all?" "Yeah, Friday's good," says Donald. "I'm free," says Michelle. "I ain't got nothing else to do," says Willie. "Alright…we'll do it then."

Jermaine turns to the band. "Welp, what do y'all want to do for the rest of the day?" "I say we go back and practice," says Donald. The rest of the band nods. Jermaine turns to Nia. "See ya tonight." Nia waves as they leave.

***

Nia closes the door and hurries back to her computer. She types "live jazz clubs in McFade City," and a list of clubs pop up. She makes a call. "Sammy's Jazz Club," the manager greets. "Do you have any spots for live music?"

***

A week later, Jermaine, Nia, Willie, Donald and Michelle are at the pizza parlor sitting at a round table getting ready to eat a cheese pizza. Each one has a slice on their plate. Jermaine holds up his slice. "A toast...to new beginnings." The tips of their pizzas touch. Wille, Donald, Michelle and Nia all take a bite while Jermaine pours parmesan cheese on his pizza.

"So, what's the surprise Nia?" Jermaine asks. "Well, I've booked y'all's first gig." Everyone is surprised. "Where?" "At Sammy's next Friday night and the payout is 500 bucks." Jermaine, Michelle, Donald and Willie look at each other in amazement.

"God is good," Donald says. "Little sis is on it," says Willie. "Nia you're the best," says Michelle. "Wait, how were you able to get us this job with no audition footage?" Jermaine asks. "I used the footage that I recorded from one of the performances that y'all did last semester." "Ah I see." "Anyway, downbeat is at eight, and y'all are done at midnight."

Everyone nods. "I also have one more surprise." They lean in to hear the news. "But y'all are gonna have to wait until the night of the gig." Willie, Jermaine, Donald and Michelle raise up their hands in a playful disappointment. Nia chuckles. "Sorry guys." "Now the suspense is killing me," says Willie.

***

Six days later...
Deborah Lee, a jazz clarinetist, is in her room practicing. She is startled when she hears something plastic hit the kitchen floor. When Deborah enters the kitchen, she notices there's a cup on the floor and her cabinet is open. She picks up the cup and puts it on the counter. She closes the cabinet.

She goes back to practice and after playing a few notes, she hears the noise again. She goes back into the kitchen but notices a different cup is now on the floor and her cabinet is open again. Fear grips her as she slowly walks backwards because she feels a presence in the room. A black armored hand with a handkerchief covers her nose and mouth from behind.

***

12 hours later...
While the garbage truck is still running, the garbage man gets out of the truck to pull out the first dumpster from the wall for emptying. When the garbage man pulls back the lid, a woman lies there on top of trash filled bags with dried blood on her chest, a treble clef carved on her forehead and her lips removed. The garbage man is shocked. He pulls out his phone. "Operator get me the police."

Later, the body is zipped up in a body bag that's on a stretcher and rolled in the ambulance by the paramedics. The entrance of the alley is taped off.

Lieutenant Pang is at the crime scene with two other policemen filling out the report on their clipboards. Detective Martinez walks under the tape and goes over to Lieutenant Pang. He speaks with a thick Puerto Rican accent, and Lieutenant Pang speaks with a thick Boston accent. "Have there been any arrests

17

Lieutenant?" "No detective, the suspect is still on the loose, and from the looks of it…we've gotta sick one on our hands."

***

Sammy's Jazz Club
Jermaine and his band are playing. The audience is really digging the music. Nia is standing by the bar. She looks over at the entrance and in comes Mr. Webb. He waves to her as he approaches her. They shake hands. "I'm so glad you can make it," says Nia. Mr. Webb looks at the band.
"Is that your brother?" "Yes." "He's smoking." Mr. Webb pulls out his phone and starts recording.

***

 Jermaine and his band end the tune. The crowd is clapping. They take their bows. Jermaine steps up to the mic. "Thank you everyone…Thank you…We are now going to our intermission…See you in 15."

They exit the stage and start mingling with the audience. Jermaine walks over to Nia. "Jermaine, I'd like to introduce you to Mr Webb. He's the A&R rep for Dixon Records." Jermaine and Mr. Webb shake hands. "It's a pleasure to meet you sir."

"Likewise…My boss is on leave, but I'll give him the video that I took of you all once he gets back. He's definitely looking to sign some new talent." "Wow!…That's so cool…I hope he likes what he sees. Mr. Webb smiles. "I think he will."

"Well I have to head out…We'll stay in touch." Mr. Webb shakes Nia and Jermaine's hand and leaves. "Wait a minute…was that the surprise—" "Yep." Nia has a smirk on her face. "Utterly amazing…How did you do it?" "He was a customer at the shop, and I invited him over."

***

Three days later, Detective Martinez and Lieutenant Pang arrive at Deborah Lee's mother's house. Detective Martinez knocks on the door. Deborah's mother opens it. "Ms. Lee?" "Yes?" "I'm Detective Martinez and this is Lieutenant Pang. We really hate to be the bearer of bad news, but your daughter has been murdered." Ms. Lee faints. Detective Martinez catches her before she hits the ground.

***

 Ms. Lee is lying on her couch. Detective Martinez is on one knee. He's fanning her while she comes to. "You went out on us," says Lieutenant Pang. Ms. Lee sits up and starts to weep. Detective Martinez and Lieutenant Pang look at each other with pity.

"Ms. Lee…I know this is difficult for you, but we need to ask you some questions," says Detective Martinez. Ms. Lee nods and gathers her composure. Detective Martinez and Lieutenant Pang pull out their pen and notepad. "Ms. Lee, when was the last time you spoke with your daughter?" Detective Martinez asks. "The last time I spoke with her was sometime last week. She was telling me about the performance she had with her band."

"Did she have a boyfriend or was seeing someone?" Lieutenant Pang asks. "The last boyfriend she had was about a year ago." "His name was umm…Floyd…Floyd Patterson." Detective Martinez and Lieutenant Pang write down the name. "What did he do for a living?" Detective Martinez asks. "He's a music teacher at TU." Detective Martinez and Lieutenant Pang continue to write down the information. "Thank you for your time Ms. Lee, and we're sorry for your loss," says Detective Martinez.

***

18

Mr. Dixon, the founder and CEO of Dixon Records, is at his desk filling out paperwork when he receives a knock on his office door. "Come in," he says in his deep, robust voice. Mr. Webb hands his phone to Mr. Dixon. "Sir, I have this video I want you to see." Mr. Dixon presses the play button and watches. "He's amazing." Mr. Dixon continues to watch. The whole group is amazing…I want to meet them. Send them an invite." "Will do sir."

***

Jermaine is at the gym hitting and kicking the heavy bag. As he takes a break, the news comes on one of the televisions. "MUSICIAN FOUND DEAD," the headline says. Jermaine becomes concerned and starts to read the closed caption. "Last Friday clarinetist Deborah Lee was found dead in a dumpster in the second alley on 13th St. Police say that she was stabbed in the heart, her lips were amputated and a treble clef music symbol was carved on her forehead. The police are investigating the murder." Jermaine looks away in disbelief.

***

Thursday Afternoon

Floyd Patterson dismissed class. As the students are walking out, Detective Martinez and Lieutenant Pang walk in. "Mr. Patterson?" Detective Martinez asks. "Yes?" "I'm Detective Martinez and this is Lieutenant Pang. There's a murder we're investigating, and we've come by to ask you some questions…Did you know a woman by the name of Deborah Lee?" He sighs. "Yes I did."

"How was the relationship between you too?" asks Lieutenant Pang. "We had a great relationship…I mean we had our disagreements like any other couple but we were able to work them out." "So you two split up on good terms?" "Yes." "Were you at beef with anyone that you think might have taken it out on her? Or do you know of any enemies that she may have had?" asks Detective Martinez.

"No I wouldn't have a clue because she was well liked by everyone." Detective Martinez nods. "No further questions…Thank you for your time."

***

Later that night…

China Fredericks, a bassoonist with the McFade Philharmonic, is walking down the sidewalk heading home from rehearsal. The neighborhood is very quiet. A black SUV with tinted windows pulls up beside her. She stops and looks at the SUV. Then the SUV stops. She turns around and briskly starts walking the other way. The door opens and shuts without the appearance of someone there. China starts to run when out of nowhere she runs into a man dressed in a black armored ninja suit. The man quickly grabs the back of her head while placing a handkerchief over her nose and mouth.

***

The next day…

Nia is taking the groceries out of the cart and putting them in the trunk of her car. Her phone starts to ring in her purse. She takes her phone out and looks at it. "MR. WEBB" shows on the caller ID. "Hello Mr. Webb!" "Nia, I have some great news. I showed Mr. Dixon the video, and he was very impressed. He would like to meet the band." "Sure!...What day works best?" "Any day next week between 8am and noon." "Ok. I'll let the band know and will get back to you."

***

Jermaine is sitting on his bed practicing his trombone when he receives a knock on his room door. He gets up and answers. "Hey, Mr. Dixon wants to meet you and the band." "Yes!" "We'll meet with him this Thursday morning at ten since we're off from school." "I'll let the band know…Dang it!" "What's wrong?" "They're playing at the workshop that day." "Well it will just be you and me…I'm going to get started on dinner."

***

Jermaine and Nia are sitting at the table. Jermaine opens up the bottle of parmesan and starts to pour it. "You're the only person I know that drowns their mac and cheese in parmesan." "That's right…They don't get no rescue tube here." Nia laughs. Jermaine smiles and goes back to eating his mac and cheese. "Jermaine…have you told the band about your abilities yet?" Jermaine sighs. "No…I'm not ready…I just want them to see me as a normal person for as long as possible." "But they're like your second family now…Don't you think—" "They'll be hurt?" Nia nods. "…That's something I wrestle with all of the time…But it's a chance I'm going to have to take."

The 6 o'clock news comes on the TV in the living room across from them. "Bassoonist China Fredericks with the McFade Philharmonic was found dead in a dumpster this morning in the second alley on 13th St. Her mutilations are identical to Deborah Lee, the clarinetist that was murdered last week except this time…a bass cleft was carved on her forehead. The police are investigating these cases." Nia turns to Jermaine. "You should help them." "Huh? Come again?" "With your abilities, you can totally help the police."

Jermaine starts to get irritated. "If I can't tell my own bandmates about my abilities, why would you think I'd be comfortable telling the police?" "You can disguise yourself." Jermaine laughs. "I'm a musician Nia…Look the police will figure it out." Jermaine dips his spoon in the mac and cheese. "But what if they don't?" "Look, I just want to concentrate on making good music…Ok?" "Ok but…you're wasting your gift." Jermaine angrily looks at Nia. "I'm done with this conversation." Jermaine gets up from the table and goes to his room. Nia is shocked.

***

Jermaine sits on the edge of his bed. He's conflicted. "I wish I didn't have these powers…" There's a knock on Jermaine's door. He gets up and opens it. "I'm sorry." Jermaine smirks. "Don't worry about it."

***

Lieutenant Pang is having a meeting with three other police officers. They are sitting at a round table. "Gentlemen, we have a Modus Operandi on our hands. Thursday night we go undercover. We'll hangout along 13th St in front of alley number two and wait for the suspect to strike. Batch one will post up from 7pm till 1am and batch two will take over the remaining 7 hours. Are there any questions?"

***

Nia punches in the code and Mr. Webb answers. "Good morning Nia. I'll let you in." They walk in and Mr. Webb meets them. "Right this way." Mr. Webb knocks on Mr. Dixon's door. "Come in." Jermaine, Nia and Mr. Webb walk in. Mr. Dixon is sitting at his desk and is on his computer. "Ah Mr. Jermaine." Mr. Dixon gets out of his chair. He shakes Jermaine's hand. Mr. Dixon looks at Nia and is immediately attracted to her. Mr. Dixon extends his hand and Nia shakes it. "Sir, this is the band's manager."

"It's a pleasure to meet you Mr. Dixon," says Nia. "Likewise…You all have a seat." Mr. Webb leaves. Jermaine and Nia walk over and take their seats in front of Mr. Dixon's desk. Mr. Dixon sits down at his desk. "Where's the rest of the band?" "They had a job at the workshop downtown," Jermaine says. "Oh yeah that is going on today…Well…I want to start off by saying I'm a fan." Jermaine and Nia smile.

20

"And I can definitely see you all being a force to be reckoned with on the jazz scene. Are you all freelance musicians?" "Yes, but we're also students at TU." Mr. Dixon grins and nods. "Good school...seniors?" "Yes...except for little sis here." "Sis?" Jermaine and Nia nod. "I'm a sophomore...studying music management." "Impressive...Well you know what they say...keep it in the family." They chuckle. "Here at Dixon Records we treat all our artists as if they are...family." "If you were to sign with us, we deduct 40% off the top, and you and your band get to keep the remaining 60% after expenses have been recouped."

"Wow 60%?" Jermaine says. Mr. Dixon nods. "We do this for all of our artists as a way of appreciating their talent." Mr. Dixon looks over at Nia in admiration. "And whatever you decide to give your manager will come out of that 60%." Nia smiles. "Do either of you have any questions for me?" "What about the masters?" asks Nia. "The masters will be released to Jermaine and his group after their contract is over. Our contract is 5 years unless the band decides to renew." Nia and Jermaine look at each other with excitement. "Mr. Dixon...I know this is off topic, but since Dixon Records has only been around for six months, what did you do before?" asks Jermaine.

"I was an engineer...creating and experimenting with advanced technology for the government. After doing that for 25 years, I retired. And decided to start a new chapter in my life with what you see here." "An engineer? That's heavy...What inspired you to start a label?" "Well my love for music and I figure why not do something to help artists succeed in this business." Jermaine nods. "You're a good man Mr. Dixon." Mr. Dixon smiles.

"Is there anything else you would like to know about me, Jermaine?" "I'm good for now." "Wonderful...Well...I would like to sign you all...What do you say?" Jermaine and Nia are elated. "...Before we sign, let us share the news with the rest of the band first," says Nia. "Fair enough." "Thank you Mr. Dixon...We'll touch base with you soon."

Jermaine and Nia get up from their chairs and head out. The portrait that's on Mr. Dixon's wall catches Jermaine's eye. Jermaine stops and stares at Mr. Dixon doing a spinning hook kick to his opponent's face. "Oh yeah, I was also a kick boxing champion." Jermaine looks back and smiles.

***

Later, Jermaine and Nia arrive at the band's apartment. Willie opens the door for Jermaine and Nia. "Come on in." "We had our meeting with Mr. Dixon, and he wants to sign us," Jermaine says. "Quit playing! Are you serious?" Willie asks. "I'm dead serious." Willie starts running in place. Donald looks down and puts his hands in his pocket. Michelle goes to high five Donald, but Donald does a quick smile and unenthusiastically gives her a high five. He puts his hand back in his pocket and looks down. Michelle is taken aback. "What's wrong Donald?"

Donald sighs. "...I hate to be the one that rains on yall's parade, but I heard some shady things about that guy." "Like what?" Nia asks. "That he likes to take advantage of people." "Really? Other musicians speak highly of him," says Nia. "Those are probably just rumors," says Jermaine. Donald still doesn't look too convinced.

"Look this is our shot Don...Don't back out now." "Yeah Donald," says Willie. "Yeah Donald," says Michelle. "Why are you just now bringing this up?" Jermaine asks. "Because I knew this would happen. Trust me I was torn because we don't have any real evidence, but at the same time I don't feel good about this...I say we wait for someone else to sign us." Jermaine, Willie, Michelle and Nia are all disappointed.

***

8:30 p.m.

Lieutenant Pang and the other three police officers drive up in unmarked cars. They park their cars on 13th St across from the second alley and are in civilian clothes. They wait.

***

10:17p.m.
A young man is holding hands with a young woman and they go into the alley. Lieutenant Pang and the three police officers text each other "*11." They get out of their cars and head to the alley. They draw their guns on the couple making out. "Freeze!" Lieutenant Pang shouts.

The man and woman stop and a dead body falls down on them. It's a young woman with a treble clef carved on her forehead and her lips amputated. The couple gasp in shock. Lieutenant Pang and the other police officers point their guns up towards the six story building. There's nothing or no one there.

***

The next day…
Nia is walking home from school. She has her phone up to her ear as it's ringing. "Hello," Mr. Dixon answers. "Mr. Dixon this is Nia." "Oh hi Nia it's good to hear from you. How are things?" "Well one of our band members has cold feet about signing." Mr. Dixon's countenance slightly drops. "Oh I see…Well you all should come to the party I'm having this Saturday at eight. This will give the band an opportunity to meet some of the other artists, and I'll personally chat with whoever is being reluctant to ease their mind."

"Sure!…That sounds great!…Thanks Mr. Dixon." "No worries…Listen, I'm going to be treating myself out to dinner this Friday night, and I wanted to see if you would like to join me?" "Oh Mr. Dixon…I'm flattered, but I don't feel it would be appropriate to take our relationship in that direction. Let's just keep things strictly business." Mr. Dixon does a quick half smile. "As you wish."

***

Jermaine and his band are at school rehearsing and come to the end of the song. "Yeah that's tight," Willie says. "Nice writing Jermaine," says Michelle. "We are definitely doing this one at our next gig." Jermaine's phone starts ringing and the band starts talking among themselves. "Hey sis." "Hey, I told Mr. Dixon how Donald was feeling." "What did he say?" "He invited us to a party he's having this Saturday. He figured this is one way to get Donald to change his mind."

"I can agree with that…Well we're still rehearsing. I'll be home soon." Jermaine hangs up. "Hey Mr. Dixon invited us to his party this Saturday." Donald becomes irritated. "You're still messing with him?" "Look Don, the man is innocent until proven guilty."

"Well my intuition says he's guilty." "How can you say that when you don't even know the guy?" "Jermaine relax…Don, you're going to have to be more open minded about this bruh," says Willie. "Don, Jermaine and Willie are right." Donald looks at the group. "Well I'm not going." Jermaine becomes furious. He grabs his trombone and case and storms out the room. Willie looks over at Donald. "See what you did man?"

***

Jermaine enters his apartment and slams the door behind him as he heads to his room. Jermaine sits on the edge of the bed. He hears a knock on his door and gets up to answer it. "Hey, is everything alright?" asks Nia. Jermaine sighs. "Donald and I got into it…He refuses to go to the party."

Nia is concerned. Jermaine goes and sits back on his bed. Nia sits next to him. "I'm gonna to start looking for a new drummer." "No. Jermaine wait…" "Don has shown he's not a team player…As much as I

22

hate to let him go…" "Jermaine, just give it some time." "That's the thing that we don't have a lot of." Nia sighs. "I totally get your point, but y'all are like family…Look give it some time and hopefully he'll come around."

***

Jermaine and his band are at the party mingling. The crowd is medium in size, but more people start to trinkle in. Jermaine gets a text from Nia that says, "Running late…Still at work…Be There Soon." As Jermaine is having a conversation with the other guests and musicians, he notices Donald walking in. "Excuse me." Jermaine leaves the group and approaches Donald. "I thought you weren't coming."

Donald chuckles. "Me too. I guess you can say I had a change of heart after thinking things over." Jermaine smiles. "I'm glad…Come on." Jermaine wraps his arm around Donald's neck as they walk to go mingle.

***

Nia writes down her last list of records and walks into the manager's office. She hands the manager the paperwork. "I'm done with the inventory." "Great, I'll see you tomorrow." Nia walks out of the store.

***

Nia arrives at her car. As she puts the key in to unlock her car door, she freezes because she feels a presence behind her. The man in the black armored ninja suit grabs her from the back and puts a handkerchief over her nose and mouth. She starts to struggle but quickly passes out.

***

Twenty - five minutes later…

Mr. Dixon walks in. He notices Jermaine and the band mingling with two of the musicians. "Good evening everyone." "Good evening Mr. Dixon," the two musicians reply. Jermaine and his band smile and wave. "I hope you all are enjoying yourselves." "Yeah we are…We're just waiting on Nia," says Jermaine. "Ah…well hopefully she'll be here shortly…Can I speak with you and the band privately?" "Sure." They walk over to a corner.

***

"I understand one of you is having some reservations about signing?" Donald raises his hand. "I'm good now Mr. Dixon." "Oh…so everyone is on the same page?" They nod. "Awesome."

***

Nia is lying on her side when she comes to. She quickly sits up and is shocked to find herself in a cage. Fear is running through her as she looks around. There's an altar.

***

The band is still mingling. "I wonder what happened to Nia," Michelle says. "Yeah me too," says Jermaine. Jermaine pulls out his phone and notices that Nia hasn't texted him again. He calls her, but he gets her voicemail. Jermaine hangs up. "I'm heading out."

***

Jermaine gets out of the Uber and goes inside the apartment. "Nia?" Jermaine closes the door behind him and turns on the light. He goes into the kitchen and turns on the light. He goes to her room and knocks. "Nia?" He opens the door.

23

***

The next morning Jermaine arrives at his parents house. "Mom, have you heard from Nia?" "Not since three days ago...Come in." Reginald comes out of the bathroom and into the living room. He's in a cheerful mood. "Hey son. What's happening?" "He's looking for Nia." "The last time we talked to Nia was a few days ago." Jermaine looks defeated. "She never showed up to the party last night." Reginald and Patricia are stunned. "This is highly unlike her," says Jermaine. "Come on, let's go ask around," says Reginald.

***

Jermaine, Reginald and Patricia arrive at Nia's friend's apartment. He knocks on the door. She opens it. "Hey Jermaine." "Hey have you heard from or seen Nia?" She looks a little confused. "The last time we talked was on Thursday...why?" "I haven't heard from her since last night." Nia's friend becomes concerned. "Oh...Well I'll call around." "While you do that I'll call the police."

***

Later, a patrol officer shows up at Jermaine and Nia's apartment. "I'm here to report a missing person's case." "Yes it's my sister." "Sister's name?" "Nia Osei." The patrol officer writes down the information. "Age?" "20." "Occupation?" "Record shop clerk and band manager." The patrol officer becomes concerned. "A female band manager huh?"

***

Detective Martinez is at his desk and on the computer. The patrol officer walks up to him. "Detective, I just took down some information on a missing person's report...The gentleman that made the report is a musician and his missing sister is his manager. They were gettin ready to sign a deal with Dixon Records. Since you're on these homicide cases, I thought this would be something you would want to look into."

***

Jermaine sits on his bed worrying about Nia. He grabs his trombone and tries to practice but can't. He lies down and eventually falls asleep.

***

Two hours pass. Jermaine wakes up. He checks Nia's room and the kitchen. He returns to his room and sits on the bed frustrated. He starts to recall the locations of the murders.

***

Jermaine walks cautiously through the alley. He scans the two dumpsters with his transparent vision. Only a few filled trash bags are there. His phone starts to buzz. "Hello?" "Mr. Osei...this is Detective Martinez..."

***

The next morning Detective Martinez arrives at Dixon Records. He rings the service bell and Mr. Webb answers. "Yes?" "Hello, I'm Detective Martinez. Is Mr. Dixon in?" "Hold on Detective." Mr. Webb goes and knocks on Mr. Dixon's door. "Come in." Mr. Webb enters and Mr. Dixon is at his desk doing paperwork.

"Sir, a detective is here to see you." Mr. Dixon looks concerned. "Tell him to come in." Mr. Webb goes back to Detective Martinez. "Detective right this way." Detective Martinez follows Mr. Webb and enters Mr. Dixon's office. "How can I help you?" asks Mr. Dixon. "Do you know a musician by the name of Jermaine Osei?" "Yes I do. Is everything ok with him?" "He hasn't seen his sister since Saturday." "Oh." As Mr. Dixon

24

and Detective Martinez continue to talk, Nia is still in the cage and in the soundproof basement beneath them.

"Did you speak with her or see her before the party?" "I sent out a mass text to her and the band reminding them about the party but that's it." "I see...Do you know if she was at odds with anyone?" "No I don't." "Thank you for your time." Detective Martinez heads to the door. "Detective...if I find anything I'll be sure to let you know." Detective Martinez nods and walks out.

Mr. Dixon pulls out Nia's phone and types, "Jermaine, I'm ok. I'm on 34th St next to the museum. Come get me." Mr. Dixon sends the text and grins.

***

Jermaine is in English literature class. His phone starts to buzz. He pulls it out and his jaw drops as he reads the text. He quickly gets up and walks down the steps to make his exit.

When Jermaine is away from the campus, he takes the back roads and runs to 34th St using his exceptional running speed. He can run up to 60 miles per hour for 30 minutes. When Jermaine gets to 34th St, he looks around.

***

Tayman University

Jermaine is sitting on a bench and Willie, Donald and Michelle are standing around him. "Man, somebody's playing with you," says Willie. "This is taking its toll on me." "Jermaine, you're not alone because this is taking its toll on all of us," says Michelle. Jermaine bows his head in distress.

***

It's raining, thundering and lightning outside. Nia is sedated and is lying on her back. Mr. Dixon, in his black armored ninja suit, puts her hands and feet in shackles. He looks at the clock on the wall and the hand strikes 7:45pm. He leaves.

***

Three hours have passed. The rain, thunder and lightning have stopped. Jermaine is in his room. He's wearing a gray long sleeve coverall. He puts on black gloves and grabs the black ski mask that's on his bed.

***

Jermaine puts on the ski mask as he walks through the alley. He scans the dumpsters with his transparent vision. Only scraps of paper are there. He climbs the fire escape ladder on the building.

***

Jermaine steps on the building top and walks a few steps while looking around. He slowly turns around and stops. Mr. Dixon is on the next building. He takes a body out of a body bag and throws the body in the alley. Jermaine quickly walks backwards. He sprints and jumps to the other building.

***

Jermaine lands. Mr. Dixon takes a body out of the other body bag and throws the body in the alley. Jermaine charges at Mr. Dixon. Mr. Dixon turns around and waits for Jermaine to get close to him. He presses the first button on his outer forearm and teleports. Jermaine becomes confused and turns around.

He is now standing face to face with Mr. Dixon. Mr. Dixon does a spinning back kick to Jermaine's abdomen. Jermaine falls to his hands and knees. Mr. Dixon does a front kick to Jermaine's lips and Jermaine falls backwards.

Jermaine gets up while being dazed. Mr. Dixon presses the second button on his forearm and turns invisible. With his hands in a boxing pose, Jermaine looks around. In his invisible form, Mr. Dixon throws a jab to each one of Jermaine's eyes. Mr. Dixon comes out of his invisible form while doing a jump spinning hook kick to Jermaine's jaw. Jermaine falls backwards and lands on the ground. Mr. Dixon mounts Jermaine and throws a punch towards Jermaine's face, but Jermaine blocks it.

Jermaine quickly puts his forearm against Mr. Dixon's Adam's apple while wrapping his other forearm around the back of Mr. Dixon's neck. Jermaine applies pressure and crushes Mr. Dixon's neck. Jermaine pushes Mr. Dixon off of him and pulls off his own mask. Jermaine pulls off Mr. Dixon's mask, and tears start to fill Jermaine's eyes.

Chapter 6

Nia is lying in bed at the hospital. Reginald, Patricia, Willie, Donald, Michelle, Detective Martinez and Lieutenant Pang are gathered around her. "What we know now is that Dixon was also some sort of idol worshiper. He had to wait until midnight on that specific night to have his way with you...and then offer you up as a sacrifice," says Detective Martinez. The countenance on Reginald, Willie, Donald and Michelle drops. "You are very lucky," says Lieutenant Pang. Reginald turns to Patricia to explain in sign language.

"...Well we have to get going...Call us if you need anything," says Detective Martinez. Detective Martinez and Lieutenant Pang leave. "We definitely have to count our blessings," Donald says. "You got that right," says Reginald..."Hey whatever happened to Jermaine?" Michelle asks.

***

Jermaine is in his bathroom. He's looking at his black eyes, busted lip and the bruise on his jaw in the mirror. "I can't let them see me like this."

To be continued...